# ARISTIDE

ROBERT TIBBER

# ARISTIDE

Illustrated by Quentin Blake

COLLINS

ARMADA LIONS

First published 1966 by
Hutchinson & Co (Publishers) Ltd, London
First published in Armada Lions 1973
by William Collins Sons and Co Ltd
14 St James's Place, London SW1

© Rosemary Friedman 1966
© Illustrations Hutchinson & Co (Publishers) Ltd, 1966

Printed in Great Britain
by William Collins Sons and Co Ltd, Glasgow

*For Louise*

This is the story of a boy called Aristide who came from France to England and of what he found there. He had to cross a big piece of deep water to get from his land to ours, but he did not come on a ship, nor in an aeroplane. He did not even have a grown-up with him.

The story begins in France.

Aristide lived with his mother, who was very beautiful, and his father, who was extremely clever, in a flat in Paris. Paris is the most important city in France. Instead of the river Thames it has the river Seine; it also has a lot of people in a hurry, shops, and cars, like any other city in the world.

All through the year Aristide went to school. He worked very hard there as all French boys do, but that is all we shall say about it because the interesting thing that happened to Aristide took place in the holidays when he went to stay with his grandmother.

Aristide's grandmother was neither beautiful (like his mother) nor clever (like his father). She was rather fat because she liked cooking and eating what she cooked. She loved Aristide very much.

On the first day of August every year the City of Paris emptied like a squeezed orange. Everybody went away for his summer holidays.

In the summer we are talking about, Aristide's mother and father left for the South of France by car, and Aristide and his grandmother hurried northwards on the train.

Aristide's mother liked the South because it was very hot and she could put on her swimsuit and rub oil on herself and stretch out in the sun like a lizard. His grandmother liked the North because

8

it was not so hot and the heat made her feel dizzy. Naturally Aristide's father followed his mother to the South because he had to rub her back with the sun-tan oil, and Aristide went with his grandmother to keep her company.

They went to a seaside called Le Touquet, and lived in a tiny villa with green shutters and frilly curtains.

Aristide liked to stay with his grandmother for the holidays, particularly because of the things they had to eat. But about his grandmother he had one complaint. It was the way she behaved on the beach.

Because Aristide's grandmother was fat she did not put on a swimsuit; because she did not want to get brown she did not rub oil on herself. This left her plenty of time to look after Aristide. She started doing it as soon as they got to the beach in the mornings. Aristide would start to dig a castle in the sand, imagining that it was a real fort with real soldiers, when his grandmother's voice would break into his dreams: 'Aristide, come and put on your hat.' No sooner had he kneeled down again before his castle with his white sun-hat on his head, than he would hear his name called once more: 'Aristide, are you hungry?' If he did not go at once to eat the roll his grandmother held out she would call again: 'Aristide, hurry up.'

Worst of all was when he went in the water.
Aristide had only to wet his big toe for his grandmother's voice to come: 'Aristide, take your rubber
ring,' and to go into the water up to his knees for
the order, this time from the edge of the sea to
where his grandmother had followed him: 'Aristide,
take care.'

And so it went on all day.

Sometimes the other people on the beach called
*their* children: Françoise! Laurent! Jean-Pierre!
Philippe! Madeleine! But the name that could be
heard over and over and over again, much louder
than the others, was 'Aristide!' 'Aristide!' 'Aristide!'

Each summer, when he went to stay with her,
Aristide's grandmother would buy him *one present*.
He was allowed to choose whatever he wanted.
Because there were so many nice things in the

shops it took Aristide a long time to make up his mind what to have. By the end of the first week, in which he looked in the shops at boats to sail and giant rubber balls and fishing-rods, he had decided that what he wanted most of all was a shiny, plastic mattress which you could blow up and float on in the sea.

Together with his grandmother Aristide went to the shop which sold them. They were hanging up outside; blue-and-white, red-and-white, and green-and-white. Some of them had a piece of clear plastic, like glass, in the pillow part, so that when you lay face down in the water you could watch the fishes swimming in the sea.

The stout lady and the small boy stood for a long time on the pavement outside the shop looking at the lovely shiny mattresses. At last Aristide said: 'Blue.' It was a big decision.

As if by magic, as soon as Aristide had spoken, the man whose shop it was came out of it and with a long stick unhooked the blue mattress from where it was hanging.

Aristide's grandmother gave the man the money. Aristide gave his grandmother two kisses, one on each cheek, to thank her for buying him the present, and carrying it together they walked through the streets to the little villa with the frilly curtains where they were to have chicken in cream for supper.

All night the shiny blue mattress lay at the foot of Aristide's bed.

The very last thing he wished before he went to sleep was that the next day would be hot enough for his grandmother to let him use it.

# 2

In the morning the sun woke Aristide. He sat up straight away and looked at his mattress.

He made his grandmother hurry with her breakfast and was cross because she had first to go to the market to buy fish for lunch.

By the time they got down to the beach most of the other children were there. They crowded round Aristide looking at the lovely mattress and saying how lucky he was. Aristide was very proud.

He could hardly wait to get changed into his swimming trunks. When he had them on he carried the mattress, which was bigger than he, into the water and laid it down on the edge. It floated beautifully. Aristide lay down on it. It bobbed up and down on the little waves . . .

'Aristide, take care!' His grandmother watched him anxiously from the edge of the water. 'Don't go out too far!'

Aristide had a wonderful morning. Each time he slipped off the mattress into the water his grandmother called, 'Aristide, Aristide, are you all right?' But he was having such fun he did not mind too much.

Aristide was cross when his grandmother said that it was time to go home and eat the fish which they had bought in the market, but she promised that they would come down to the beach again in the afternoon.

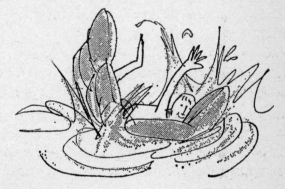

They had fish (fried in butter till it was golden), green beans, Camembert cheese (Aristide's favourite), and wine to drink. When they had finished they both felt sleepy so they had a little rest.

Then they went down to the beach.

Aristide carried the mattress down to the sea, not knowing that this was to be the beginning of his great adventure.

What happened was this:

At the same moment as Aristide put his shiny blue-and-white mattress in the water and lay down on it, flat on his tummy, Aristide's grandmother had one of her dizzy spells.

She was standing up folding Aristide's clothes away neatly into her striped beach bag, when she felt very odd indeed and fell back into her deckchair. The people on the beach gathered round

and spoke to her but she did not open her eyes.

*And so it was that nobody saw Aristide go into the water on his mattress.*

And Aristide was far too busy to notice what was happening on the beach.

He lay on his tummy, looking through the little plastic window to see if he could see any fish. The hot sun was making his back warm and he was very comfortable. Because he could not see any fish and he wanted badly to see some, Aristide put his hands in the water and paddled along a little to see if he could find some in a different spot.

He was so happy, so warm, and so busy looking for fish through the little plastic window that it

was a long time before he realised that he could not hear his grandmother's voice calling 'Aristide! Aristide!'

He lifted his head from the little plastic window where he was watching for fish to see why it was so quiet. What he saw gave him a big surprise.

He seemed to be in the middle of the ocean.

A long way off he could see the beach.

It was very peaceful.

It was very warm.

It felt very nice (the sea rocked the mattress like a baby's cradle), and Aristide did not mind at all. He felt so happy that he laid down his head on the little plastic window and he *went to sleep*.

While Aristide floated happily away the people on the beach tried to make Aristide's grandmother open her eyes. When she did not they sent for an ambulance.

The ambulance took her to the hospital.

At the hospital Aristide's grandmother woke up but the doctor said she *must not talk*. He gave her some medicine so that she would sleep soundly all night and feel quite well in the morning.

*And so it was that nobody looked for Aristide or knew that he was far, far out at sea on his mattress.*

When Aristide woke up it was dark and he was
very cold. For a moment he could not remember
where he was. Then he did. He was far, far out at
sea on his new, shiny blue mattress.

Aristide looked around him and what he saw
made him feel afraid. The sea was very big and
very black and he could not see the end of it; the
sky was very big and very black and he could not
see the beginning of it, he was all alone, very small,

in the middle of the bigness and the blackness. He was cold, he was hungry, he was thirsty. He began to cry, and his tears felt warm on his cold face. The mattress was going up and down because the waves were quite big. Aristide clung on tightly so that he would not fall off into the deep, dark water.

Then he noticed the stars shining out brightly from the black sky, some large and twinkling, and some not so bright, and suddenly he stopped crying.

The reason he stopped crying was this.

Aristide's clever father not only knew what was going on in the world but he also knew what went on in the sky and about the stars. He had told Aristide that if he remembered the names of all the stars and where they were in the sky he would never be lost at night but would always be able to find his way home.

So Aristide looked carefully up into the big, black sky.

It was quite a long time before he found what he was looking for. It was a large, bright star in the middle of some smaller ones. It was called the Pole Star. Aristide knew that if he paddled his mattress *away* from the star it would lead him back to his grandmother.

This made him feel much better. He put his

hands carefully over the sides of the mattress into the icy water and moving them backwards and forwards made it move along quite fast away from the Pole Star. He no longer felt afraid.

But Aristide's troubles were not over.

When he had gone a little way over the bumpy waves a cloud suddenly formed in the black sky

and hid the Pole Star from sight. At the same time a little breeze jumped up so that the waves became much larger. They became so large that they *turned the mattress round in the water.*

Aristide paddled very hard indeed. He longed to reach home so that he could have something to eat and to get dry, and to hear his grandmother once again call 'Aristide! Aristide!'

He seemed to be moving along well.

He did not know that he was going in the *wrong direction*.

He wasn't going home to France at all.

He was making straight for England.

Poor Aristide.

It was the fault of the cloud for hiding the Pole Star.

All through the long night Aristide paddled and paddled and paddled. By the time the darkness melted away and it began to be morning his hands were so cold from the water that they felt as if they did not belong to him. Also his arms ached. He longed not to move them any more but he knew that if he did not move his mattress along he would never get to land but would stay in the middle of the ocean for ever more.

Aristide watched the sun climb, like an orange ball, up into the sky.

He lifted his head from the mattress and saw that *not far away was land*.

Aristide was so happy that he forgot he was tired and cold and hungry and that his arms ached. He made the mattress move so fast towards the land that he thought was France, but which was really England, that soon he could see the beach, wide and empty in front of him. He saw some sea-weed and some rocks and a house with a pointed roof.

It was not a beach that he knew. Certainly not the beach he had been to every day with his grandmother. Aristide was so glad to see any beach at all though, so that he would not have to stay in the middle of the ocean, that he did not mind a bit.

After a few moments more of working very hard, Aristide put his hands over the sides of the mattress.

They touched the sand at the bottom of the water.

He was safe!

A largish wave washed him right up with a rush on to the sand and left him there. It was funny to be quite still on his mattress, not going up and down any more. Aristide lay there for a bit just enjoying the feeling.

Then he got off the mattress.

But he was so stiff from lying on his tummy all night long, and from being cold and wet, that he fell right down again. He couldn't stand up. He couldn't even get back on to the mattress! So he lay on the sand with the water tickling his feet and waited.

He closed his eyes.

When he opened them again he found a small boy a little older than himself standing over him and staring at him. The boy had red hair and

freckles on his face. He was pointing a gun at
Aristide.

For a while the two boys looked at each other,
then the boy with the red hair opened his mouth
to speak. To Aristide's surprise he spoke in
English.

Aristide could speak English quite well. He had
learned it from his clever father, who spoke it very
well, and from his mother, who was not clever but
knew enough to come to England for the week-
end to do some shopping.

But because the boy with the red hair spoke
very fast indeed and because Aristide had been
expecting him to speak in French and because
he was very tired as he had not slept all night he

did not understand at first what was said to him.

What the boy with the red hair had said to Aristide was:

'Don't-move-or-I'll-shoot!'

He said it again and pointed his gun fiercely at Aristide.

'Don't move or I'll shoot.'

Aristide stared at him.

'Stand up. Hands above your head and tell me your business,' the boy said, still pointing the gun.

Just then another boy with a turned-up nose climbed over the rocks.

He saluted the boy with the red hair.

The boy with the red hair saluted back.

'This is my second-in-command,' he said to Aristide, pointing to the boy with the turned-up nose.

'Who is he?' the boy with the turned-up nose said, pointing to Aristide.

'I don't know. I just found him when I was on patrol.'

'He might be a spy.'

'He might be.'

'We'd better take him prisoner.'

'We'd better.'

'On your feet!' the boy with the red hair said to Aristide who was still lying on the sand.

When Aristide took no notice he said it again, this time very crossly.

'ON YOUR FEET!'

'Look!' the boy with the turned-up nose said, pointing at Aristide, 'he's crying!'

And indeed he was. Cold and miserable and hungry, and not understanding what was going on,

Aristide felt very sad indeed. He wanted his grandmother.

'Perhaps he's wounded,' the boy with the red hair said, lowering his gun.

'He doesn't seem able to talk,' the boy with the turned-up nose said.

'I don't think he can walk either.'

28

'We'd better get a stretcher party,' the red-haired boy said firmly.

'Can't we use this mattress?' the boy with the turned-up nose said pointing to the blue-and-white shiny mattress with the little plastic window that had brought Aristide all the way from France to England.

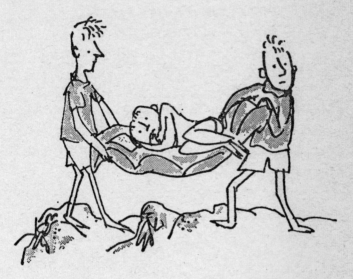

'I suppose we could.'

And so together the two boys lifted Aristide once more on to his mattress, and each taking one end of it they climbed carefully over the rocks, trying not to slip into the puddles, towards the house with the pointed roof that Aristide had seen from the sea.

They did not take him into the house though, but into a big white tent which was at the bottom of the garden.

As they opened the flap of the tent and struggled to get the mattress through without dropping it the most wonderful smell he had ever smelled came to Aristide.

It was the smell of frying sausages.

A small boy was cooking them in a pan over a stove in the tent.

When he had been laid with a bump on the ground Aristide stared longingly at the sausages.

'I think he's hungry!' the boy with the red hair said. 'Cook, give the prisoner something to eat!'

The boy who was in charge of the sausages put two on a plate and gave them to Aristide.

They were very hot indeed as they had just come out of the frying-pan but in a moment they had gone.

The boys stared at him.

'You'd better give him some more,' the boy with the red hair said, watching his breakfast disappear.

They gave Aristide all the sausages. He ate fifteen in five minutes.

'Well!' the boy with the turned-up nose said, 'What shall we do with him now?'

'We'll have a conference,' the boy with the red hair said. 'Call the others.'

Two more small boys came in from outside the tent.

All the small boys huddled together in the corner of the tent to talk about Aristide.

When they turned back to tell him what they had decided they found that he was asleep.

'Well!' the boy with the turned-up nose said. 'That's that!'

'He's shivering,' the boy with the red hair said. 'Bring one blanket each!'

The boys did as they were told and the boy with the red hair covered Aristide, who had on only his swimming trunks, with five blankets. He

tucked them in round the mattress. Aristide was
dreaming of fish fried golden in butter, of green
beans and of Camembert cheese.

# 4

Aristide slept on his mattress covered with the five blankets *all day*.

Every so often the boys who had found him came into the tent to see if he had woken up. But he slept and he slept and he slept.

The boys were sitting in the tent eating their supper of beans from a tin when Aristide opened his eyes.

At first he thought he was still at sea. Then he realised that he was no longer cold and wet and that he could not be.

Next he thought that he must be at home in his bedroom in the flat in Paris. Then he remembered he had been staying with his grandmother in Le Touquet so he knew he could not be.

After that he decided that he must be in his grandmother's villa with the green shutters and the frilly curtains.

Then he saw the boys eating their supper and he remembered that he did not know where he was at all.

'He's awake!' the boy with the red hair said. 'Look!'

All the boys stopped eating their beans and turned to look at Aristide.

'Hallo,' the smallest of the boys said. He was the one who had cooked the fifteen sausages that Aristide ate for breakfast.

He sounded friendly.

'Hallo!' Aristide said.

'Are you feeling better?' the boy with the turned-up nose said.

Now that he had had a good sleep and was no longer tired Aristide remembered his English.

'Yes, thank you.'

'What's your name?' the little cook said.

'Aristide,' Aristide said, eyeing the beans.

'Where do you live?'

'Paris.'

The boy with the red hair who was a little older than the others said:

'But that's in France!'

Aristide nodded his head.

'Then you're *French*,' the boy with the red hair said.

Aristide nodded again.

They all stopped eating.

'How did you get here?'

Aristide pointed.

'On a mattress!'

'All the way from France!'

'Wasn't it terrible out at sea?'

'Weren't you afraid of drowning?'

'Why did you come?'

'Haven't you any people or anything?'

Aristide's head turned from one to the other.

'Am I in France?' he said, speaking English in a very funny way.

They stared at him.

'Of course not.'

'You're in England.'

'England?'

'Of course.'

'It is not possible,' Aristide said.

'Why?'

'Because of the *stars*. My father told me about them.'

'You must have got them muddled up,' the boy with the red hair, who was a Boy Scout, said.

Aristide shook his head.

'I remembered as my father told me.'

'Then he must have told you wrong.'

'My father is very clever.'

The boys saw that it was useless to argue with Aristide. They asked him about crossing the sea

'Was it cold?' they said.

'And wet?'

'And dark?'

'Were you afraid?'

'Did you see any fish?'

'Were the waves big?'

They stared at him with admiration.

Aristide got off the mattress and stood up in the tent.

'Where are you going?' the boy with the red hair said.

'Home.'

'You can't go home!'

'Why?'

'Because you are our prisoner. Sit down and have some supper.'

Aristide was very hungry because he had been asleep all day so he sat down on the mattress again and ate the beans they gave him.

'I don't know what the "Greens" will say when they hear we've got a real prisoner,' the boy with the turned-up nose said. 'A French one, too.'

'Don't be silly,' the boy with red hair said. 'We shan't tell them. We shall have to hide him.'

'How can we do that?'

'Keep him in the tent.'

'All day?'

'Yes. We can take him out at night,' the boy with the red hair said.

'A sort of secret weapon?'

'In a way. We shall find a use for him. He may sway the balance.'

Aristide looked from one to the other not understanding the difficult words. He had finished his beans and he felt sleepy. He lay back on the mattress, pulled the blankets over him and went back to sleep.

'Well,' the boy with the red hair said. 'He's the sleepiest prisoner I've ever seen!'

'What shall we do?' the boy with the turned-up nose said.

'Nothing. We shall have to leave his interrogation until the morning. Keep guard on the prisoner,' the boy with the red hair said. 'I'm going up to the house for provisions.'

'Are you going to tell them?' the boy with the turned-up nose said.

'About him?' The boy with the red hair pointed at Aristide, fast asleep.

'Yes.'

'No,' the boy with the red hair said firmly.

'Don't you think you ought?' the little cook said.

'I will on Sunday. If we tell them before Sunday they might take him away or something and that will cut down our numbers. He's a priceless prisoner.'

'But . . .' the little cook began, but the boy with the red hair wouldn't let him finish.

'Silence!' he said very crossly. 'I'm the captain.'

So the little cook had to keep quiet and the boy with the red hair opened the flap of the tent and crossed the garden towards the house with the pointed roof.

In the house with the pointed roof lived the mother and father of the boy with the red hair, the boy with the turned-up nose, and the little cook.

They were all on holiday; the mother and the father and the three boys and two more small boys who were their cousins. They had already been at the seaside for a month. As they had only two more days left the boys had asked their father if he would allow them to live by themselves in the big tent at the bottom of the garden for the days that were left. They had promised to be very careful and the mother and father had promised that they would not look in the tent and interfere but would let the boys do whatever they liked as long as they were good. The big tent was white.

In the next door garden there were some other boys. They had asked their mother and father if they could do exactly the same thing.

Their tent was green.

The boys in the white tent had declared war on the boys in the green tent.

They called themselves the "Whites" and the "Greens".

When the boy with the red hair arrived at the house with the pointed roof for more food his mother said: 'Are you sure you're all right down there in the tent?' and gave him some bread and some cheese and some fruit cake.

And the boy with the red hair said: 'Of course.'

'Not too cold?' his mother said.

'I hope you aren't getting up to mischief,' his father said.

'Have you enough blankets?' his mother said.

The boy with the red hair thought of Aristide, their extra guest.

'It is a bit cold,' he said.

His mother gave him two more blankets.

'Don't you think I ought to come and see if you're comfy?' she asked.

The boy with the red hair was horrified.

'Oh no,' he said. 'We're quite all right. I have to go now.'

'Are you looking after my baby?' his mother said. She meant the little cook who was the youngest.

'Of course,' the boy with the red hair said.

'Don't make him do all the dirty work,' his mother said.

The boy with the red hair looked pained as if he would not dream of doing such a thing.

Then he said good night to his mother and father and left before they asked him any more questions.

In the morning they ate the bread and the cheese and the fruit cake for breakfast.

The boy with the red hair said to Aristide: 'I'm David. This is Mark.' He pointed to the boy with the turned-up nose. 'And this is John.' He pointed to the little cook. 'And these are our cousins Charles and Henry.' The two other boys smiled at Aristide.

They finished their breakfast and Mark, who was about the right size, lent Aristide a windcheater as Aristide had only his swimming trunks and although it was summer time it was rather cold even in the tent.

'Right,' David said when they were all ready. 'I'm going to interrogate the prisoner.'

Mark and John came to Aristide's side and to his surprise pulled him up from his mattress where he had been sitting comfortably and led him to David who was sitting with a pencil and notebook on an upside-down box in the corner of the tent.

The cousins, Charles and Henry, sat on their sleeping bags and watched.

'Ready?' David said, pushing the red hair sternly out of his eyes.

The boys nodded and Mark scratched his turned-up nose.

'Name?' David said, getting his pencil ready to write.

'Aristide,' Aristide said, surprised because he had already told David his name.

'Surname?' David said.

'You know, like Smith or Jones or Brown,' Mark said helpfully.

'Silence,' David said. 'I'm doing the talking. It doesn't matter anyway. "Aristide" is long enough for both.' He wrote 'Areesteed' in his notebook. It took up a whole line.

'Date of birth?'

Aristide did not understand.

'Born,' David said. 'When is your birthday?'

Aristide understood.

'*Janvier*,' he said, which is the French way of saying January.

This time David did not understand.

'Do you think that's summer or winter?' he asked Mark. And then to Aristide:

'What's the weather like on your birthday?'

'It always snows,' Aristide said, thinking of the white flakes falling softly outside the big windows of the flat in Paris.

'Date of birth, winter,' David wrote in his notebook.

'Mother's name?' David said.

'Marie-Hélène,' Aristide said very quickly.

David couldn't spell it so he put down an X.

'Father's name?'

'Dominique.'

David put down another X.

'Why did you come here?' David said.

'It was a mistake,' Aristide said. 'My mattress brought me.'

44

'Are you a spy?'

'No,' Aristide said. He did not know what a spy was but he was beginning to enjoy the game. It was more interesting than playing on the beach with his grandmother.

'Will you help us in the war?' David said.

'Where is the war?' Aristide looked round.

'We are at war with the boys in the next garden. The battle is tomorrow night.'

Aristide shook his head.

'Why do you shake your head?' David said.

'Because I will not help you in the war,' Aristide said.

David looked surprised. 'Why on earth not?'

'Because war is bad.'

'Who says so?'

'My father.'

'But everybody has wars all over the place.'

'I know. People get killed. Children too . . .'

'Ours is only a pretend war,' David said. 'You can't kill anyone with sand bombs, plastic rockets and water pistols.'

'My father says people must understand each other,' Aristide said, 'then there will be no more war.'

'This is a very small war,' David said. 'Only boys playing.'

Aristide shook his head.

David sighed. 'It's only the boys in the next garden.'

'But I do not know the boys in the next garden,' Aristide said. 'Why should I fight them?'

'Because I say so,' David said. 'And I am the captain. Everyone obeys the captain. Besides you are our prisoner and you must do what I tell you.'

'But why must you fight?' Aristide said.

'To see who is the strongest,' David said.

'Does it matter?' Aristide said.

'Of course,' David said. 'If we win, next year everyone will want to come in our tent.'

'I think you are silly,' Aristide said.

'Then you must be a coward.'

'A coward?' Aristide said, not understanding.

'Afraid of fighting,' David said.

'I am not afraid. I just think it's silly.'

'Well, since you are the only one who doesn't like fighting, it must be you who is silly. It's all arranged and we are looking forward to it. You will help, won't you?'

'No, I will not,' Aristide said.

'All right, then,' said David, who was getting a bit fed up. 'Will you at least help us to make our ammunition?'

'What is that?' Aristide said.

'Bombs,' David said. 'Made out of sand wrapped in paper bags. We need hundreds and hundreds.'

'All right,' Aristide said.

David was surprised that he agreed so quickly but he did not know about the plans Aristide was making in his head to stop the war.

The next day they got ready for the battle which was to be at midnight.

They took a big pile of brown paper bags they had collected and went down to the beach. There they filled the bags with sand, finishing them with a twist so that they had bombs to throw at the Greens. Farther down the beach, past the break-water which stretched out to sea, the Greens, led by the big boy, were making bombs to throw at them. As fast as David and Mark and John and Aristide made the bombs, Charles and Henry carried them across the beach and over the rocks and through the garden and piled them up behind the tent. They worked so hard that by the time lunch-time came the mound of bombs made out of sand was almost as high as the tent.

David said that was enough.

For lunch they had spaghetti from a tin and Aristide thought it was horrible.

'Don't you eat spaghetti in France?' Charles asked.

'Yes, but not from a box,' Aristide said.

'You mean a tin. Do you eat frogs?'

'Yes.'

'And snails?'

'Sometimes,' Aristide said.

'Tell us what else,' David said.

Aristide thought for a moment. France seemed very far away.

'Start with breakfast,' David said to help him.

'Croissants,' Aristide said.

'What on earth's that?'

'Little breads,' Aristide said.

'He means "rolls",' Mark said. 'Go on.'

'Jam,' Aristide said, 'and coffee.'

'Coffee?' John said.

Aristide said, 'Of course.'

'Good lord, how foul. What else?' They were all very interested.

'That's all,' Aristide said.

'No eggs, or bacon, or sausages?'

'In the morning!' Aristide said. 'No.'

'I'd be starved to death,' Henry said. 'What about lunch?'

'Fishes,' Aristide said. 'Meat, green beans or little peas and some cheese.'

'What about pudding, roly-poly or treacle tart?'

Aristide shook his head. 'No.'

'Poor you,' John said. 'Is it true the children drink wine?'

'Of course,' Aristide said.

'Is it nice?'

'Why not?'

They were getting tired of talking about food.

'I'd like to go to France,' David said. 'I wonder what frogs taste like.'

In the afternoon they made their uniforms. David walked up to the village and bought some white crepe paper. He brought it back to the tent and showed them how to cut it into squares and fold it to make into helmets and belts to tie round their waists.

'We shall be able to see each other easily in the dark,' he explained.

'What time are we starting?' Henry asked.

'We open fire at midnight,' David said. 'By then it will be properly dark.'

'Suppose we don't stay awake,' Henry said.

'We shan't bother. We shall go to bed early and get up again at twelve. Then we will be fresh.'

'Who will wake us?' John said anxiously.

'I am going up to the house to get the alarm clock out of the kitchen, then we shan't have to worry.'

David had thought of everything.

By six o'clock they were all ready.

In the tent they checked their plastic rockets,

to make sure that they were working, and filled their water pistols with water from the sea. Then they filled buckets with water so that they would not have to keep going down to the sea during the battle.

By eight o'clock they were all in bed feeling very

excited indeed about the battle that would not be long in coming.

'Now all go to sleep,' David commanded, 'and I shall wake you at midnight. Good night everyone.'

'Good night, Captain,' they said.

Then they all turned over in their sleeping bags and made themselves comfortable and went to sleep.

*Except for Aristide who stayed awake.*

*Aristide was thinking.*

# 7

Aristide was thinking about his plan to stop the war.

The plan was this.

There was a big shed at the bottom of the Whites' garden. In it Aristide was going to hide all the boys' clothes, and their weapons, and their uniforms. After that he was going to spill all the sand from the bombs they had made so carefully so that there would be nothing to throw at the Greens. This was not all.

He was going to do exactly the same to the Greens.

With no clothes and no uniforms and no bombs how could there be a war?

He waited until it was quite dark then very carefully, making less noise than a mouse, he crept over to where David was sleeping with the clock beside him.

Nobody moved.

The time on the clock which had hands which shone in the dark was half past ten.

An hour and a half until midnight.

Aristide wondered if all the boys were asleep.

He kicked somebody's shoes to make a small noise.

Nobody stirred.

In the darkness he put on his swimming trunks and the windcheater the boys had lent him and set to work.

It took him more than an hour.

Back and forth and back and forth to the potting shed with the clothes and the uniforms and the weapons. Then he started on the bombs, emptying all the sand from the paper bags until he had quite a large pile.

When he had finished he was very tired but he

still had to do exactly the same with the Greens' things. Taking David's torch he crept into the Greens' garden and into their tent.

They were all sound asleep waiting for midnight.

Then he carried away the five silver shields they had made so that they could recognise each other in

the dark.

After that he dealt with their weapons.

Then he got rid of their bombs.

When he had finished, the potting shed was almost full and there was a big pile of sand outside the Greens' tent.

Aristide was very tired indeed.

His job was finished.

Now there was only one thing left **to do**.

He crept into his own tent, put back the torch he had borrowed next to David, took his blue-and-white mattress and carried it down to the dark beach.

On the beach he sat on his mattress, hidden behind a large rock and waited to see what would happen.

Aristide did not have long to wait.

He had only a few moments of looking out on to the dark beach and listening to the water thumping its waves on to the shore, when from behind the rock where he was hidden he heard the alarm clock in the Whites' tent.

A minute later he heard an alarm clock ring in the Greens' tent.

Because it was quiet on the beach the bells sounded very loud.

In the Whites' tent all the boys were sitting

up because they had been woken by the alarm bell.

'Into battle!' David said.

And they leaped out of their sleeping-bags and looked for their clothes.

'I can't find my clothes!' Mark said.

'Hey. Somebody's pinched my pullover!' John said.

'My shorts have gone!' Charles said.

'So have my plimsolls,' Henry said.

And then they realised that *none* of them had anything to put on.

'The Greens must have come in and taken our clothes while we were asleep,' David said. 'Never mind. We shall still win the battle.'

'In our pyjamas?' Charles said, shivering.

'Why not?' David said. 'Pick up your weapons and put on your helmets.'

Then they discovered that their weapons and the helmets they had made so carefully had gone.

Then they looked out of the tent and found that the mound of bombs had gone.

And it was Mark who said: 'I say, where's Aristide?'

And they discovered he too had gone.

'I say,' David said, now really angry. 'The Greens have taken our prisoner too. We shall just have to go and get everything back.'

'I'm cold,' Charles said.

'Well jump up and down,' David said unsympathetically. 'We're all in the same boat.'

In the Greens' tent exactly the same thing was happening.

They were all standing in the tent shivering.

They were sure that the Whites had come in while they slept and had taken all their things.

The big boy who led them said they must go over to the Whites and take everything back.

So it was that from behind his rock where he was hiding on his blue-and-white mattress Aristide saw a very funny sight indeed.

From the Whites' garden crept five little boys in pyjamas.

From the Greens' garden crept five little boys in pyjamas. It was too dark to see their faces.

The Greens walked softly over the beach towards the Whites and the Whites crept softly over the beach towards the Greens.

Suddenly they saw each other, just white shapes in the darkness, and they all stood still.

'Where are our clothes and our bombs?' David called across the beach.

'Where are *our* clothes and *our* bombs?' the big boy who was the leader of the Greens called back.

'We haven't touched your things,' David shouted.

'And we haven't touched your things!' the big boy shouted back.

'You're lying!' David called.

'I'm not!' the big boy called back.

'I don't believe you,' David said. 'We're coming to look in your tent.'

'And we're coming to look in yours,' the big boy said.

And all the boys ran towards each other.

They met in the middle of the wide stretch of dark beach.

David raised his arm and grabbed what he thought was the hair of one of the boys from the Green tent.

'Ouch!' Mark said. 'What did you do that for?'

'Sorry,' David said. 'I thought you were a Green.'

The big boy who led the Greens picked up some sand and threw it at what he thought was one of the Whites.

It landed on his own second-in-command.

All the boys chased each other round the beach.

Mark pinched Charles and John kicked Henry.

The Greens all kicked and pinched each other.

It was impossible to see who was who in the darkness.

From behind his rock where he was watching Aristide laughed and laughed and laughed at the sight of ten small boys in striped pyjamas running over the sand trying to catch the wrong people.

It looked very foolish indeed.

Suddenly there was a shout from the bottom of the Whites' garden and a beam of bright light lit up the stretch of beach where the boys were chasing each other.

'What's going on?' a grown-up voice called.

All the boys stood still.

Mr. Bainbridge, the father of David and Mark and John, came on to the beach in his dressing-gown holding a big torch.

Nobody answered him.

'What are you doing out here in your pyjamas in the middle of the night?' Mr. Bainbridge said, looking at the boys, who felt very stupid and not like brave warriors at all. 'David, please explain!'

'Well,' David said, 'we were going to have a

battle but the Greens took our clothes and our helmets and our sand bombs . . .'

'No we did not!' the big boy who led the Greens said. 'David and his lot took our clothes and our shields and our bombs . . .'

'He's lying!' David said.

'Silence!' David's father said. 'You'd better all come here while we sort this out.'

They all gathered round and Mr. Bainbridge said: 'David, what have you done with the Greens' clothes?'

'I haven't touched them,' David said.

'On your honour?' Mr. Bainbridge said.

'On my honour,' David said, and Mr. Bainbridge knew that he was telling the truth because he had brought him up to do so.

Then the big boy who led the Greens promised that he too hadn't touched the Whites' clothes.

And they looked at each other in amazement.

Then little John thought of Aristide.

'It must have been Aristide!' he said.

'Aristide!' David said and he asked the Greens if they had taken their prisoner.

The Greens promised that they hadn't.

'Well, where is Aristide?' David said.

'Who is Aristide?' David's father said.

'Our prisoner,' David said. 'He must have run away.'

'I've just remembered,' Mark said. 'His mattress wasn't in the tent.'

'Good gracious!' Charles said. 'You don't think . . .?'

'Quick,' David yelled, waving his arms. 'Follow me!'

Mr. Bainbridge, who was very puzzled because he did not know what was going on, followed the boys to the edge of the water.

'Look!' David said.

All the boys and Mr. Bainbridge looked to where David was pointing.

He was pointing out to sea.

The lazy moon had just got up. By its light they saw, quite far away, a tiny figure floating on a mattress.

Then the excitement started.

'What is it?' Mr. Bainbridge said, staring at the tiny speck on the water.

'Aristide,' David said.

'Our prisoner,' Mark said.

'Do you mean to say there's a *boy* out there?'

'A French boy,' David said patiently. 'Aristide.'

'Good heavens!' Mr. Bainbridge said. 'We must get the coastguards. He'll drown!'

'Oh no, he won't,' said David. 'He's on his mattress.'

'A mattress?' Mr. Bainbridge said. 'At this time of night? Where does he think he's going?'

'Back to France, I suppose,' David said, but his father was already running as hard as he could back to the house to telephone the coastguards.

The coastguard soon fetched Aristide and his mattress back to the beach where Mr. Bainbridge was waiting with the boys.

'This is my father,' David said to Aristide when he had climbed out of the boat.

Aristide gave a little bow and held out his hand to Mr. Bainbridge. (French boys are always polite even when their feet are wet.)

David's father shook hands with Aristide.

'Where did you think you were going?' he said.

'Home,' Aristide said. 'My grandmother will be wondering where I am.'

'If you come with us,' Mr. Bainbridge said, 'you can go home to France in an aeroplane. It will be much quicker than your mattress.'

'All right,' Aristide said. He wanted very much to go home.

In the big kitchen of the house with the pointed roof, David's mother gave them all blankets to put round their shoulders and made some cocoa for Aristide and the boys and the coastguard who had gone out in his boat to rescue Aristide from the middle of the ocean.

She kept saying: 'Poor little thing, poor little mite,' and going 'tut-tut-tut' every time she looked at Aristide.

While they were drinking the cocoa Mr. Bainbridge said: 'I am terribly angry with you, David,

for not telling anybody about Aristide. He has been here for two days. Don't you think his mother and father will be worried about him in France? They must be going out of their minds.'

Mrs. Bainbridge made some more 'tutting' noises very loudly.

'I was going to tell you after the battle,' David said. 'We were *going* to tell you.'

'I can't believe that any child of mine could be so stupid,' Mr. Bainbridge said. 'I must telephone the police immediately!'

When the cocoa was finished a very fat policeman, who looked as if he had just got out of bed, came round to ask Aristide some questions.

He could hardly believe that Aristide had come all the way from France on a mattress and that he had been in the tent for two days without anyone knowing.

The fat policeman called Aristide his 'little man'

and asked him questions very slowly so that he would be able to understand, about where he lived and the name of his mother and father and his grandmother and a great many other questions until Aristide was so weary he just could not answer any more but kept yawning and yawning.

Then the fat policeman put away his pencil and his notebook and gave Aristide one last look as if he could not believe his eyes, and went back to the police station.

Mrs. Bainbridge took Aristide upstairs and gave him some pyjamas belonging to Mark and put him into a big, comfortable bed.

She tucked him up tightly and kissed him on his forehead.

By the time she had put out the light and closed the door gently Aristide was fast asleep and dreaming that he was on the sea going up and down with the waves on his mattress.

Aristide slept until lunch-time the following day.
He was woken by a very great weight squashing
him so that he could hardly breathe.

He opened his eyes to see what it was.

To his surprise he found his grandmother sitting
on his bed.

'Aristide, Aristide,' she was saying and smothering him with kisses at the same time. 'Aristide, my
little cabbage.'

'Grandmother,' Aristide said, speaking in French
because his grandmother did not understand
English. 'What are you doing here?'

'I came immediately in an aeroplane,' Aristide's grandmother said, also in French, 'as soon as we heard from the police that you were in England. Your mother and father are downstairs.'

'Are they angry with me?' Aristide said.

'Angry!' Aristide's grandmother said. 'I do not think you can ever realise what you have done to them. To all of us. Everybody in the whole of France has been looking for you.'

Suddenly Aristide realised what a dreadful thing it was that he had done. He began to sob.

Aristide's grandmother cradled him in her arms as though he were a baby.

'Why did you run away, Aristide?' she said. 'Weren't you happy in the little villa at Le Touquet? Didn't we have lovely things to eat?'

'Yes, Grandmother,' Aristide said. 'I didn't mean to run away. I just floated away on my mattress.'

'What a terrible time you must have had,' Aristide's grandmother said.

'Oh no,' Aristide said. 'I enjoyed it very much.'

Just then Aristide's beautiful mother came into the room.

She was very brown from all the sun and the oil she had rubbed on herself as she lay on her mattress on the beach in the South of France. But she

looked as if she had been crying and crying and crying.

It made Aristide feel very ashamed.

Aristide's grandmother got off his bed to make room for his mother who was not a quarter as heavy and smelled very nice indeed. She did not say anything but just hugged him and hugged him and hugged him and cried some more on to his pillow. Aristide's bed was getting very wet indeed with all the tears.

A voice from the door said: 'Now what's all this noise?' And it was Aristide's clever father, and his beautiful mother went out of the room blowing her nose on a tiny lace hanky and left the two of them together.

Aristide's father did not cry.

He kissed Aristide on both cheeks and said: 'It is good to see you.' Which made Aristide feel even worse than his grandmother's smothering and his mother's crying.

'I think that it was very clever of you to cross

from France to England on your mattress,' Aristide's father said. 'Weren't you afraid?'

'I found the Pole Star like you told me,' Aristide said. 'I thought I could find my way home. Then a cloud hid the star and I went in the wrong direction. I did not mean to come to England on my mattress.'

'I'm sure you didn't,' said Aristide's father, 'but when you found you were in England why did you not tell someone so that we could come and fetch you straight away?'

'Because of the war,' Aristide said. 'There was to be a war between the boys and I wanted to stop it.'

'And did you?' Aristide's father said, interested.

'Yes, I took away all their clothes and their weapons. In the dark they could not tell who were friends and who were enemies. They all looked the same.'

'We are all the same,' Aristide's father said. 'It was very clever of you to stop the war. But you should have told someone where you were. You have put a lot of people in France to a great deal of trouble looking for you.'

'I am very sorry,' Aristide said. 'I did not mean to.' Aristide's father kissed him again on both cheeks, then he helped him to get dressed and they both went downstairs for the lunch that Mrs. Bainbridge had been cooking.

While they were eating, David's father talked to Aristide's father and David's mother to Aristide's mother. Aristide's grandmother just sat there enjoying the steak and kidney pudding which she had never eaten before but which she thought was very good indeed.

When they had finished eating, Aristide's father said that it was time for them to go.

Before they left, Aristide's father invited David to come and spend a holiday with Aristide in Paris. Both the boys were very pleased they were not saying good-bye for ever.

Aristide's father had a car outside and into it got Aristide and his mother and his grandmother.

As they drove away down the little road they all turned round to wave at Mr. and Mrs. Bainbridge and David and Mark and John and Charles and Henry and the boys from the Green tent who had come to say good-bye to Aristide.

There really was quite a big crowd.

Later that night Aristide and his family arrived at the Airport in London to get a plane back to France.

At the Airport it was quite exciting. There were men with cameras and ladies with notebooks and a lot of people seemed very interested in Aristide. They took photographs of Aristide saying how it was on the mattress and of his mother looking

beautiful but tired and of his grandmother crying.

It was quite dark by the time they got on to the aeroplane.

The aeroplane rose very swiftly like a majestic bird up and up and up into the black sky.

Aristide looked out of the window next to his

seat and watched the lights of the Airport twinkling like stars below.

In no time at all they were over the deep, dark sea and Aristide looked affectionately up at the luggage rack over his head on which was his shiny blue-and-white mattress, folded flat into a neat square.

# The Reluctant Dragon

### KENNETH GRAHAME

'I *can't* fight and I *won't* fight. Besides, I haven't an enemy in the world,' the dragon announced firmly.

And he did so want a peaceful life. To write sonnets and find a place in Society was all he asked. So why did the whole town insist that he battle with St George, who was such a nice fellow anyway?

# The King of the
# Copper Mountains

### PAUL BIEGEL

For more than a thousand years King Mansolain has reigned over the Copper Mountains, but now he is old and tired. To keep his heart beating, he must hear exciting stories.

So one by one the animals of his Kingdom come to tell their tales – the fierce wolf, the chattering squirrel, and the three-headed dragon, breathing fire. The beetle sits close to the King's ear to tell his story while the other animals lie on his beard. Next comes the mighty lion and last of all, the dwarf. He prophesies that the old King *could* live a thousand more years, but only if the Wonder Doctor arrives in time. . .

# Parsley the Lion

### MICHAEL BOND

'Dill,' Parsley read, 'is a dog. He is modest . . . kind . . . a loyal friend . . . noble . . . upright . . .'

Parsley read Dill's entry for 'Who's Who' again, because it *certainly* wasn't the same dog he knew! The Dill that Parsley knew had sold him that dud car with three wheels and only a reverse gear – the same dog who pretended he owned the only television in the Herb Garden!

No, Dill definitely wasn't 'modest, noble' and all that. In fact, Parsley thought the description suited himself much better!

*Parsley Parade* is also an Armada Lion.

# Parsley Parade

### MICHAEL BOND

Parsley gave a start. 'You mean, you can actually *see* something?'

'Yes,' said Dill. 'A tall, dark figure with silken whiskers. A handsome devil if ever I saw one.'

'Let *me* have a look,' Parsley exclaimed as Dill stood up.

'I'm afraid it's gone now,' said Dill sadly. 'I think I must have been looking at my own reflection.'

'I need patience when you're around,' growled Parsley. 'And as for this crystal ball. If you ask me, there's no future in it.'

*Parsley the Lion* is also an Armada Lion.